# The
# United Nations

# Global Leadership

# UNICEF and Other Human Rights Efforts

## Protecting Individuals

by Roger Smith

Mason Crest Publishers

Philadelphia

Mason Crest Publishers Inc.
370 Reed Road
Broomall, Pennsylvania 19008
(866) MCP-BOOK (toll free)

First printing
1 2 3 4 5 6 7 8 9 10
          Library of Congress Cataloging-in-Publication Data

Smith, Roger, 1959 Aug. 15-
  UNICEF and other human rights efforts : protecting individuals / by Roger Smith.
      p. cm. — (The United Nations—global leadership)
  Includes bibliographical references and index.
  ISBN 1-4222-0069-8  ISBN 1-4222-0065-5 (series)
  1. Human rights. 2. United Nations. 3. UNICEF. I. Title. II. Series.
  JC571.S653 2007
  341.4´8—dc22
                        2006001311

Interior design by Benjamin Stewart.
Interiors produced by Harding House Publishing Service, Inc.
www.hardinghousepages.com
Cover design by Peter Culatta.
Printed in the Hashemite Kingdom of Jordan.

# Contents

# Introduction
## by Dr. Bruce Russett

The United Nations was founded in 1945 by the victors of World War II. They hoped the new organization could learn from the mistakes of the League of Nations that followed World War I—and prevent another war.

The United Nations has not been able to bring worldwide peace; that would be an unrealistic hope. But it has contributed in important ways to the world's experience of more than sixty years without a new world war. Despite its flaws, the United Nations has contributed to peace.

Like any big organization, the United Nations is composed of many separate units with different jobs. These units make three different kinds of contributions. The most obvious to students in North America and other democracies are those that can have a direct and immediate impact for peace.

Especially prominent is the Security Council, which is the only UN unit that can authorize the use of military force against countries and can require all UN members to cooperate in isolating an aggressor country's economy. In the Security Council, each of the big powers—Britain, China, France, Russia, and the United States—can veto any proposed action. That's because the founders of United Nations recognized that if the Council tried to take any military action against the strong opposition of a big power it would result in war. As a result, the United Nations was often sidelined during the Cold War era. Since the end of the Cold War in 1990, however, the Council has authorized many military actions, some directed against specific aggressors but most intended as more neutral peacekeeping efforts. Most of its peacekeeping efforts have been to end civil wars rather than wars between countries. Not all have succeeded, but many have. The United Nations Secretary-General also has had an important role in mediating some conflicts.

UN units that promote trade and economic development make a different kind of contribution. Some help to establish free markets for greater prosperity, or like the UN Development Programme, provide economic and technical assistance to reduce poverty in poor countries. Some are especially concerned with environmental problems or health issues. For example, the World Health Organization and UNICEF deserve great credit for eliminating the deadly disease of smallpox from the world. Poor countries especially support the United Nations for this reason. Since many wars, within and between countries, stem from economic deprivation, these efforts make an important indirect contribution to peace.

Still other units make a third contribution: they promote human rights. The High Commission for Refugees, for example, has worked to ease the distress of millions of refugees who have fled their countries to escape from war and political persecution. A special unit of the Secretary-General's office has supervised and assisted free elections in more than ninety countries. It tries to establish stable and democratic governments in newly independent countries or in countries where the people have defeated a dictatorial government. Other units promote the rights of women, children, and religious and ethnic minorities. The General Assembly provides a useful setting for debate on these and other issues.

These three kinds of action—to end violence, to reduce poverty, and to promote social and political justice—all make a contribution to peace. True peace requires all three, working together.

The UN does not always succeed: like individuals, it makes mistakes . . . and it often learns from its mistakes. Despite the United Nations' occasional stumbles, over the years it has grown and moved forward. These books will show you how.

*UNICEF saves the lives of children around the world.*

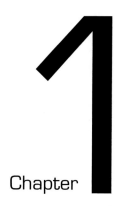

Chapter **1**

# UNICEF

In the past, many Afghan children died from measles, that nation's number-one killer disease. In 2002, however, that changed. Throughout the nation, loudspeakers at the mosques proclaimed, "Free measles vaccines today! Come to the mosque with your children now!" Local officials in Afghanistan teamed up with UNICEF, the United Nations Children's Fund, to immunize most Afghan children between the ages of six months and twelve years.

# UNICEF and Other Human Rights Efforts: Protecting Individuals

Vaccinations are just a tiny part of the work of UNICEF: the organization helps children in 158 countries and territories providing health care and nutrition, safe water and sanitation, basic education and protection of mothers and infants. The official mission of UNICEF is "to promote the survival, protection, and development of all children worldwide." Two of its goals are "Health for All" and "Water and Sanitation for All."

## History

UNICEF began as a response to the suffering of children caused by the Second World War. About fifty million people died in World War II, and the newly formed United Nations recognized that many children in Europe were suffering after the war. Children lacked food, medicine, and clothing; some children, especially babies, were dying of disease and starvation. In response to this crisis, the United Nations created a special agency for children. At first, it was called the International Children's Emergency Fund (ICEF). ICEF provided dried milk and vaccinations to the children suffering from the war. In 1953, ICEF became a permanent part of the United Nations and changed its name to UNICEF.

## The Declaration of the Rights of the Child

An important UN document that states the organization's commitment to human rights for children is the Declaration of the Rights of the Child. This includes the following principles:

**Declaration of the Rights of the Child**
*Whereas* mankind owes to the child the best it has to give, *Now therefore, The General Assembly Proclaims* this Declaration of the Rights of the Child. . . .
*Principle 1*
The child shall enjoy all the rights set forth in this Declaration. Every child, without any exception whatsoever, shall be entitled to these rights, without distinction or discrimination on account of race, colour, sex, language, religion, political or other opinion, national or social origin. . . .
*Principle 2*
The child shall enjoy special protection, and shall be given opportunities . . . to develop physically, mentally, morally, spiritually and socially. . . .
*Principle 3*
The child shall be entitled from his birth to a name and a nationality.

### Principle 4
The child shall enjoy the benefits of social security. He shall be entitled to grow and develop in health. . . . The child shall have the right to adequate nutrition, housing, recreation and medical services.

### Principle 5
The child who is physically, mentally or socially handicapped shall be given the special treatment, education and care required by his particular condition.

### Principle 6
The child, for the full and harmonious development of his personality, needs love and understanding. He shall, wherever possible, grow up in the care and under the responsibility of his parents. . . .

### Principle 7
The child is entitled to receive education. . . . The child shall have full opportunity for play and recreation. . . .

*Each child in the world is entitled to a name and a nationality.*

*Children deserve to grow up protected from racial discrimination.*

*Principle 8*
The child shall in all circumstances be among the first to receive protection and relief.
*Principle 9*
The child shall be protected against all forms of neglect, cruelty and exploitation. He shall not be the subject of traffic, in any form.
*Principle 10*
The child shall be protected from practices which may foster racial, religious and any other form of discrimination.

# Funding for UNICEF

It is costly to fund UNICEF's efforts to aid children throughout the world. Most UNICEF funding comes from the governments of the UN's member nations, and individual and group donations from around the world also help out. In the United States, volunteers and workers with the U.S. Fund for UNICEF work to help reach funding goals for the organization. They visit schools and teach about the programs of UNICEF. They also raise money by selling UNICEF greeting cards.

One way children get involved in fund-raising for UNICEF is the "Trick or Treat for UNICEF" program. This program first began on Halloween of 1950 when some children in Philadelphia carried decorated milk cartons from house to house to collect coins for poor children overseas: that year they raised just $17. Since then, however, trick-or-treaters for UNICEF have raised more than $188 million for the organization.

# Organization

The executive board, made up of thirty-six members who serve three-year terms, runs UNICEF. Seats on the board are divided up by regions of the world: Africa gets eight members, Asia seven, Eastern Europe four, Latin America together with the Caribbean five, and Western Europe, Japan and the United States twelve.

The directions of the executive board are put into action by the secretariat, run by the executive director. The first executive director was Maurice Pate, who served from 1946 to 1965.

*UNICEF provides vaccinations to children, protecting them from disease.*

## Immunizations and Childhood Diseases

After World War II, ***tuberculosis (TB)*** threatened the survivors of war, especially children. TB was called "the white plague" because the disease gave victims a very pale color. In 1947, the Red Cross began to vaccinate children in Europe, and they asked UNICEF to assist. It was the largest vaccination program ever attempted, and it was the start of UNICEF's work to improve the health of children around the globe.

Over the past five decades, UNICEF has provided vaccinations for children around the globe, making some parts of the world free from certain diseases. The Caribbean and Latin America have not seen a new case of ***polio*** in more than a decade, and China was likewise declared polio-free in 2001. UNICEF today is working in Angola and the Democratic Republic of the Congo to rid those countries of polio as well.

## Nutrition and Hunger

No one likes to think about hungry children. When we see commercials for relief agencies that show us rail-thin boys and girls, we may turn the channel—or maybe we decide to give money to the organization. At any rate, we go about our daily business and soon forget that somewhere people are hungry. Unfortunately, in many parts of the world, people cannot "turn the channel" on their hunger, nor can they ever forget it. And yet freedom from hunger is one of the most basic of human rights.

Since UNICEF began, one of its priorities has been feeding children. In war-ravaged Europe in the 1940s and in Africa in the 1950s, malnutrition was common. As a response, UNICEF provided dairy products, of which the United States had a surplus at the time.

Though its early efforts were effective, UNICEF has not always done a perfect job combating malnutrition. In the 1950s and '60s, UNICEF relied on the results of a study claiming that global malnutrition was mostly the result of too little protein. Therefore, the United Nations spent time and money at food production plants in Algeria, Chile, Guatemala, and Indonesia grinding soybeans, peanuts, fish, and oils into special high-protein mixtures. Unfortunately, the resulting products were expensive and tasted horrible. Then, after all that work, experts found the earlier study was wrong: lack of protein wasn't the main problem in worldwide malnutrition. The real problem was simply lack of adequate amounts of locally produced food in much of the world, so UNICEF began working harder to improve local food production.

## School in a Box

Earthquakes, fires, and hurricanes can wipe out schools—but UNICEF attempts to bring learning to children even in the worst situations. Since 1990, UNICEF has been supplying "schools in a box." One box can hold everything needed to school eighty children. These boxes, packed at UNICEF's Copenhagen warehouse, are also called "edukits." The kit contains a paint and brush to turn the box lid into a blackboard: it also holds pens, a clock, books, chairs, and posters with letters, numbers, and multiplication tables. For students, the box has crayons, pencils, erasers, a pencil sharpener, rulers, and scissors. An edukit may not contain a school like yours, but it can hold everything necessary to provide children with a basic education in an emergency. In 2001, nineteen thousand edukits reached children in areas where natural disasters had removed their schools.

*Africa has 12 million AIDS orphans.*

In Somalia, half a million people were hungry in 2005. Drought and war have kept food scarce. UNICEF distributes high-protein biscuits and specially treated milk for Somali children. They did the same for Iraqi children in 2003. Fourteen million people in the Horn of Africa spent much of 2002 lacking enough food and water, although only a year before, UNICEF and nongovernmental organizations (NGOs) had worked hard to prevent *famine* in that area. UNICEF responded to the emergency by providing mass quantities of a high-nutrition mixture called Unimix, which contains corn, beans, oil, and sugar. Although UNICEF and other organizations work tirelessly to raise awareness and provide food, thousands of children still starve to death around the world each year.

## AIDS

Since 1981, more than 25 million people have died from AIDS. The disease may be passed on from an infected mother to her unborn child; it is also spread through sexual contact or by using an infected needle. It first enters the bloodstream as a virus called HIV, and many people live a long time with HIV without coming down with the often-deadly AIDS.

In 2005, some 40.3 million people around the world lived with HIV/AIDS. Almost 5 million people contracted the disease in the same year, and more than 3 million died from the disease. Young people (15–24 years old) account for half of all new HIV infections worldwide, and more than 6,000 become infected with HIV every day. Africa has 12 million AIDS orphans.

UNICEF educates young people in epidemic-stricken nations about the ways HIV/AIDS spreads. One way UNICEF does this is through peer discussion groups, where young people in a nation can help others to protect themselves from contacting the disease. Some UNICEF AIDS programs provide testing so people can know if they are infected, and provide condoms to help protect sexually active teens.

## Providing Safe Water

You probably don't think much about clean water. We assume we can turn on the tap at anytime and get water to drink or wash things in. However, for millions of people in developing countries, lack of clean water is an everyday struggle. Cholera and other diseases and conditions like diarrhea result from dirty water and poor sanitation. Cholera is a disease that attacks stomachs and intestines, and it can be deadly. For well-fed and healthy people, diarrhea is just an inconvenience. However, for people already weakened and malnourished, diarrhea can prove deadly. Poor sanitation happens when communities lack ways to remove human and animal waste and keep water supplies clean.

Around the world, more than 1 billion people lack safe drinking water. This is so, despite the fact that in most parts of the world there is clean, unpolluted ***groundwater*** available beneath communities. Poor communities may lack access to clean groundwater because they don't have an affordable means to bring the water to the surface. UNICEF programs provide hand pumps that are inexpensive to install and maintain, which are friendly for the environment. A hand pump can be positioned right over a village well; it does not require electricity or gas to operate. In twenty years, more than one billion people in over forty nations have gained access to clean, safe water by means of hand pumps.

Sometimes, disasters cause a shortage of water. An earthquake in 2001, for instance, damaged water and sanitation systems in Gujarat, India. In response, UNICEF set up more than 3,400 tanks to hold water temporarily. The same year, earthquakes in El Salvador left 700,000 people without safe water as the earthquakes destroyed water and sanitation systems. UNICEF drove in trucks full

*The 2005 earthquake in Pakistan destroyed water and sanitation systems, as well as homes and lives.*

*People in Africa may need to travel miles to a safe water source.*

of water and provided chlorine to treat wells and water systems. In 2002, after a cease-fire from war in Angola, millions of people were at risk from lack of clean water. Once again, UNICEF stepped in to help; in this case they provided pipes, pumps, cement, and advice so that communities could set up clean drinking and sanitation systems.

## Education

In the 1970s, UNICEF began thinking about ways to help provide education for poor children in developing nations. Children in rural areas often do not have the chance to go to school that urban children have: they often have to help their family or community by earning a living. In some countries, literacy (the ability to read and write) was actually dropping. UNICEF knew something had to be done. Today, UNICEF allocates 20 percent of its program budget to education, especially the education of girls.

UNICEF looked at a successful experiment in Colombia's rural schools. In these areas, teachers and books were in short supply, so the *Escuela Nueva* (New School) program grouped teachers and students together as needed to make supplies stretch; teachers stressed the most practical skills needed for students to find work in their communities. Between 1985 and 1989, UNICEF worked with the Colombian government to expand schools in rural areas; as a result, they added ten thousand new schools in half a decade, and this enabled Colombia's children to gain reading and writing skills rapidly.

In some nations, constant warfare and threatened violence prevent children from going to school. In 2002, in Angola, a million children were unable to attend schools. Warfare had destroyed school buildings and supplies, and caused a lack of trained teachers. UNICEF organized training programs that trained 1,500 teachers and assistants for children in refugee camps. They also helped start mini-school programs to provide basic reading and writing skills for twenty thousand refugee children, and provided learning materials for 120,000 children in the area.

*Senegalese children attend a UN-built school.*

## Women's Rights

Throughout its history, UNICEF has been concerned for the rights and health of mothers and babies. Issues of concern have been making childbirth safer and the right to breastfeed infants. In the past few decades, UNICEF workers realized they needed to assist women in areas other than motherhood. In the developing world, women work as educators, mothers, farmers, workers, and community leaders; one-third of households in developing nations are headed by women, and yet women still face unequal treatment and abuse.

One area of special concern to UNICEF is female genital abuse (FMG). In certain cultures, it is customary to cut girls' bodies in their private areas—their genitals. FMG has no medical benefit, and it robs girls of their dignity and makes them ashamed to be female: in short, it is abusive. UNICEF workers, along with many people around the world, are actively opposing this practice.

## Child Refugees

From its founding, UNICEF has worked to help children in emergencies. This is still an important goal for the organization today. Children who are refugees or *internally displaced* persons face many challenges. They often crowd together in camps, and such crowding causes danger of sickness and shortages of food or water. UNICEF sends kits of special supplies to these camps.

When UNICEF hears of a refugee situation or other disaster, its warehouse staff in Copenhagen, Denmark, sets quickly to work preparing emergency response kits: it has twenty-nine different kits for different situations. These are usually prepared within twenty-four hours and shipped out to their destinations. In 2001, UNICEF shipped more than seventy-five thousand emergency response kits to eighty-four different countries.

Life in refugee camps is not easy. Children live in crowded tents with other family members. They have to use *latrines* used by many other people. They have to wait in line for everything they need to live: water, food, firewood, or medical care. In some cases, people are refugees for only a few weeks, but in other cases, they have to wait until a war is over or a political situation is settled. UNICEF works to make these difficult situations as livable as possible.

However, UNICEF is not the only part of the United Nations concerned with human rights. The protection of human rights is central to the UN's entire indentity.

*Around the world, children's human rights are particularly at risk.*

Chapter **2**

# The UN Charter
# and the UN's Role
# in Human Rights

I magine you are Amerigo, a thirteen-year-old boy living in the South American nation of Ecuador. You live alone on the streets, working at any job you can get. You are always hungry, and you do not know where you will be able to sleep safely each night. Or suppose you are Maya, a girl living in the same country. You used to go to school, but your parents decided they could not pay the money required for your education. You were very sad when you had to leave school; now you work hard every day to support your family. You don't think this is fair, because your parents still pay for your brothers to get an education; they believe boys need an education more than girls do.

# UNICEF and Other Human Rights Efforts: Protecting Individuals

These sorts of problems are common for children around the world. The rights of health, safety, and education are among the rights of children declared by the United Nations. They are rights the United Nations says everyone in the world should have—so we call them "human rights."

Since 1945, the United Nations has worked to promote and protect human rights around the world. Some people have praised the United Nations, others have made fun of it, while others have attacked it; nations have used the organization for both good and bad goals. For more than six decades, the United Nations has attempted to make peace, provide aid for people who suffer, and guarantee rights to all the world's citizens, but it has often been unable to achieve those goals. At the same time, the United Nations holds a unique position that sometimes enables it to succeed in bringing about peace and human rights.

## The UN Charter

You have probably learned in school about the Constitution of the United States (or Canada, if you live there); the founders of a nation write a constitution when their nation is born. It contains important ideas they hope the country will follow as long as it exists. Nations are not alone in having constitutions: when companies or other groups form, they create documents that explain who they are and what they will do. The UN Charter is a sort of "constitution" for the United Nations. According to the *Oxford English Dictionary*, another word for "charter" is "written constitution."

The word "charter" usually refers to someone or something giving rights or powers to a group of people. For example, in the Magna Carta, written in 1215, the king of England promised certain rights to the English people. In the UN Charter, the people of the world granted themselves the rights, powers, and responsibilities listed in the charter.

The ideas and rules contained in the UN Charter apply to all its member states. The United Nations in 2005 includes 191 member states, nations that work together for their common good. Fifty nations signed the UN Charter in San Francisco on June 26, 1945. The charter contains 19 chapters and 111 articles. It begins with the expression, "We the peoples of the United Nations."

## History Behind the UN Charter

Most constitutions or charters contain older ideas—previous documents inspire the people who write new charters. The UN Charter is no different. Its history reaches back at least a century or more.

For as long as people have existed, they have warred against one another and violated each

*The flags of the UN's member nations*

## The Preamble to the United Nations Charter

*We the Peoples of the United Nations Determined*

to save succeeding generations from the scourge of war, which twice in our lifetime has brought untold sorrow to mankind, and

to reaffirm faith in fundamental human rights, in the dignity and worth of the human person, in the equal rights of men and women and of nations large and small, and

to establish conditions under which justice and respect for the obligations arising from treaties and other sources of international law can be maintained, and

to promote social progress and better standards of life in larger freedom,

*And for these Ends*

to practice tolerance and live together in peace with one another as good neighbors, and

to unite our strength to maintain international peace and security, and

to ensure by the acceptance of principles and the institution of methods, that armed force shall not be used, save in the common interest, and

to employ international machinery for the promotion of the economic and social advancement of all peoples,

*Have Resolved to Combine our Efforts to Accomplish these Aims*

other's rights. After more than half a million Europeans died in wars in the early nineteenth century, nations gathered together to form the Congress of Vienna in 1815, the first global peace meeting. The Vienna Congress made agreements that helped European nations keep peace between them for almost a century. However, the peace agreements of Vienna fell apart with the First World War. World War I caused more than 20 million deaths; the world had never seen such horrors.

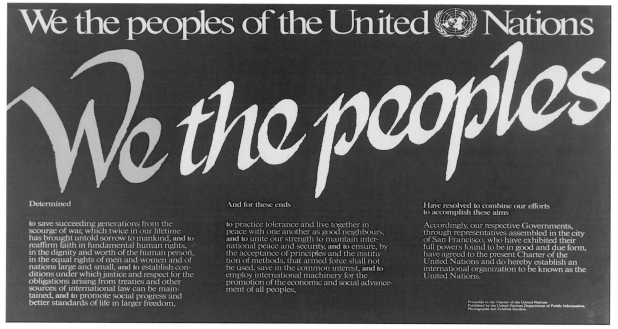

*The UN Charter*

Reacting to the horrors of the World War I, President Woodrow Wilson of the United States led the movement to create a new organization called the League of Nations. The basis for President Wilson's plan was an article titled "The League of Nations: A Practical Suggestion," by General Jan Smuts of South Africa. This article expressed the belief that "civilization is one body and . . . we are all members of one another." Founders organized the League of Nations around a document titled the Covenant of the League of Nations. The primary goal of the League of Nations was to use discussion as a means to settle disputes between nations, but the covenant did not include the term "human rights."

Ironically, President Woodrow Wilson's nation, the United States, doomed the League of Nations when the U.S. Congress refused to join. After World War I, people in the United States favored the idea of *isolationism*. They thought the United States would be better off avoiding involvement with other countries.

As World War II began, people around the world discussed ideas for a replacement to the League of Nations. In 1941, nations that were warring against Germany gathered at St. James'

*England's Winston Churchill, America's Franklin Roosevelt, and the Soviet Union's Joseph Stalin agreed on the UN charter in 1945.*

# Chapter Two—The UN Charter and the UN's Role in Human Rights

Palace in London and signed a document called the Inter-Allied Declaration. It promised they would work together to promote worldwide freedom and peace. This beginning led four years later to the United Nations. The basic shape of the UN charter came from the *Allied* governments during World War II. (These included the United States, England, and the Soviet Union.) President Franklin Roosevelt in 1942 first used the expression "United Nations" when referring to those nations that united their forces to oppose Nazi Germany and Imperial Japan in the Second World War.

While the war was still going on, U.S. Secretary of State Cordell Hull formed a committee to come up with ideas for a new international organization. In August 1943, he presented a paper titled "Charter of the UN"; for the next two years, people reviewed and changed the proposed charter. In October of 1943, China, the United Kingdom, the United States, and the Soviet Union agreed that the world needed a new international organization to guide the nations toward peace after the war. During the summer of 1944, representatives of those four countries met in Washington, D.C., to work on the charter for this new organization, and Winston Churchill (England) Franklin Roosevelt (United States), and Joseph Stalin (Soviet Union) agreed on its most important ideas at the Yalta Conference in February of 1945.

The conference that founded the United Nations took place in San Francisco in June 1945. At the conference, all the nations that had declared war on Germany and Japan prior to 1945—fifty-one nations in all—were invited to help finish writing the UN Charter. They agreed that the charter would become official as soon as the five permanent *Security Council* members (the United States, the United Kingdom, China, the USSR, and France) plus a majority of other members agreed to it. The charter was officially approved on October 24, 1945—now known as United Nations Day—when all member nations had signed it.

The preamble (opening words) of the UN Charter say it is an agreement not among "governments" or "countries" but between "the peoples" of the world. It emphasizes the need for peace, human rights, and better living standards around the globe, saying the United Nations will "reaffirm faith in fundamental human rights, in the dignity and worth of the human person, in the equal rights of men and women and of nations large and small." Chapter I of the charter speaks of encouraging the rights and freedoms of people and nations. It also says the United Nations will work "to achieve international cooperation in solving international problems of an economic, social, cultural, or *humanitarian* character, and in promoting and encouraging respect for human rights and for fundamental freedoms for all without distinction as to race, sex, language, or religion."

*All people have the right to a decent standard of living.*

# Chapter Two—The UN Charter and the UN's Role in Human Rights

## The UN's Role in Human Rights

For sixty years, the United Nations has worked to guarantee rights for all people. These rights include the right to vote, the right to a decent ***standard of living***, the right to be free, the right not to suffer torture or cruel punishment, and the right to be free from ***discrimination***.

Human rights include the right of independence; that is, the peoples of the world have the right to live under a government they choose. One important UN goal is helping colonies become independent nations. When the United Nations began in 1945, more than half the people of the world did not enjoy this right because they were colonies of other nations. (Colonialism is the practice of a nation ruling another nation; the people of colonial nations do not choose their laws or the form of government that rules them—another nation forces these on them.) The United Nations does not decide the form of government that a nation should follow once the nation gains independence; rather, the United Nations makes sure the people of the freed nation choose for themselves the form of their new government.

Human rights include freedom from discrimination. This means no one should treat another person differently or unfairly because of his or her race, sex, language, or religion. In the past, when state governments in the United States did not allow African Americans to vote, sit with people of other races in restaurants or on buses, or live and work where they wished, these were denials of basic human freedoms.

Human rights also include "the right to freedom of movement and residence within the borders of each state. Everyone has the right to leave any country, including his own, and to return to his country" (UN Universal Declaration of Human Rights, Article 13). Nations violate these rights when they force people to be refugees. People become refugees because of war, lack of food, or fear of torture within their own country. These circumstances force them to leave the place where they live and move elsewhere, often leaving behind supplies and belongings they need for survival. In the twenty-first century, millions of people are refugees.

Human rights do not change from nation to nation. Each person on the earth, young or old, male or female, rich or poor, has the right to certain privileges.

Chapter

# The Universal Declaration of Human Rights

How do you know what your rights are in your school or in your home? An authority—your teacher or your parent—defines rights and responsibilities and tells you what those are. You probably have a list of rules posted in your classroom. Your teacher or the school principal designed these rules to make sure all students enjoy their rights, such as the right to learn in the classroom and the right to be free from bullying.

*The Convention on the Rights of the Child seeks to protect the civil rights of children around the world.*

# Chapter Three—The Universal Declaration of Human Rights

The United Nations has attempted to do the same sort of thing for the nations of the world. The most important document that explains global human rights is the Universal Declaration of Human Rights (UDHR), which members of the United Nations adopted in 1948.

## Development of the Universal Declaration of Human Rights

For most of history, tribes, kingdoms, or nations made up the rules that established what was fair for their members. As humans became more and more organized, larger and larger units chose the rules for their members. However, there was no worldwide agreement as to what rights should be shared by all the world's citizens.

Before World War II, no one had attempted to make up a worldwide list of what human rights should be. (Religions attempt to do that, but the peoples of the world follow different religions, so spiritual beliefs have not created global agreement regarding human rights.) There were some agreements between several nations regarding human rights, such as European agreement to ban slavery in 1815. The Hague Convention of 1907 established rules governing the ways nations could treat citizens of other nations, but it said nothing about the mistreatment of citizens in their own countries.

The Universal Declaration of Human Rights is rooted in a speech made by U.S. president

## The Convention on the Rights of the Child

Throughout its history, the United Nations has passed many declarations concerning the well-being and rights of children worldwide. However, these declarations are not enforceable. To better protect the needs of all children, the United Nations passed the Convention on the Rights of the Child in 1989. This is the first legally binding international tool that can be used in protecting all of the civil rights of children. UNICEF uses this convention to guide its work.

The convention consists of fifty-four articles and two optional protocols. According to the UNICEF Web site (www.UNICEF.org):

Every right spelled out in the Convention is inherent to the human dignity and harmonious development of every child. The Convention protects children's rights by setting standards in health care; education; and legal, civil and social services.

# UNICEF and Other Human Rights Efforts: Protecting Individuals

Franklin D. Roosevelt in 1941. President Roosevelt was troubled by the actions of the Nazis in Germany, who committed some of history's most awful human rights abuses. In his speech, Roosevelt defined four basic human freedoms: freedom of expression, freedom to worship, freedom from want, and freedom from fear.

The San Francisco Conference that established the United Nations also created a commission to define "human rights," and in 1946, the Commission on Human Rights began working on the UDHR. The chairperson for the commission was Eleanor Roosevelt, the wife of President Roosevelt. Other important members were John Humphrey of Canada, Peng-chun Chang of China, and Frenchman René Cassin. In 1968, the Nobel Prize Committee awarded Cassin the Nobel Peace Prize for his work on behalf of human rights, including the drafting of the UDHR.

## Difficulties in Agreeing on Human Rights

There are two reasons why it has been difficult reaching worldwide agreement about human rights. First, nations do not want other nations telling them what to do. Second, different cultures disagree as to what "rights" should be guaranteed.

After the United Nations was established, critics said that its ideas about human rights expressed the beliefs of Western nations rather than a truly global, *multicultural* view. Western

## Other UN Human Rights Resolutions

There are other UN Human Rights Resolutions that do not fit into any of the categories above; smaller agencies with the United Nations wrote most of these. Examples include:

- the Conventions on Elimination of all Forms of Racial Discrimination (1966)
- the Suppression and Punishment of the Crime of Apartheid (1973)
- the Political Rights of Women (1953)
- the Suppression of the Traffic in Persons (1950).
- the Eradication of Hunger and Malnutrition (1974)
- the Rights of Disabled Persons (1975)
- the Rights of Persons Belonging to National, Ethnic, Religious and Linguistic Minorities (1992)

*Franklin D. Roosevelt was concerned with basic human freedoms.*

# IN CONGRESS, JULY 4, 1776.

# A DECLARATION

## BY THE REPRESENTATIVES OF THE

# UNITED STATES OF AMERICA,

## IN GENERAL CONGRESS ASSEMBLED.

WHEN in the Course of human Events, it becomes necessary for one People to dissolve the Political Bands which have connected them with another, and to assume among the Powers of the Earth, the separate and equal Station to which the Laws of Nature and of Nature's God entitle them, a decent Respect to the Opinions of Mankind requires that they should declare the causes which impel them to the Separation.

We hold these Truths to be self-evident, that all Men are created equal, that they are endowed by their Creator with certain unalienable Rights, that among these are Life, Liberty, and the Pursuit of Happiness—That to secure these Rights, Governments are instituted among Men, deriving their just Powers from the Consent of the Governed, that whenever any Form of Government becomes destructive of these Ends, it is the Right of the People to alter or to abolish it, and to institute new Government, laying its Foundation on such Principles, and organizing its Powers in such Form, as to them shall seem most likely to effect their Safety and Happiness. Prudence, indeed, will dictate that Governments long established should not be changed for light and transient Causes; and accordingly all Experience hath shewn, that Mankind are more disposed to suffer, while Evils are sufferable, than to right themselves by abolishing the Forms to which they are accustomed. But when a long Train of Abuses and Usurpations, pursuing invariably the same Object, evinces a Design to reduce them under absolute Despotism, it is their Right, it is their Duty, to throw off such Government, and to provide new Guards for their future Security. Such has been the patient Sufferance of these Colonies; and such is now the Necessity which constrains them to alter their former Systems of Government. The History of the present King of Great-Britain is a History of repeated Injuries and Usurpations, all having in direct Object the Establishment of an absolute Tyranny over these States. To prove this, let Facts be submitted to a candid World.

He has refused his Assent to Laws, the most wholesome and necessary for the public Good.

He has forbidden his Governors to pass Laws of immediate and pressing Importance, unless suspended in their Operation till his Assent should be obtained; and when so suspended, he has utterly neglected to attend to them.

He has refused to pass other Laws for the Accommodation of large Districts of People, unless those People would relinquish the Right of Representation in the Legislature, a Right inestimable to them, and formidable to Tyrants only.

He has called together Legislative Bodies at Places unusual, uncomfortable, and distant from the Depository of their public Records, for the sole Purpose of fatiguing them into Compliance with his Measures.

He has dissolved Representative Houses repeatedly, for opposing with manly Firmness his Invasions on the Rights of the People.

He has refused for a long Time, after such Dissolutions, to cause others to be elected; whereby the Legislative Powers, incapable of Annihilation, have returned to the People at large for their exercise; the State remaining in the mean time exposed to all the Dangers of Invasion from without, and Convulsions within.

He has endeavoured to prevent the Population of these States; for that Purpose obstructing the Laws for Naturalization of Foreigners; refusing to pass others to encourage their Migrations hither, and raising the Conditions of new Appropriations of Lands.

He has obstructed the Administration of Justice, by refusing his Assent to Laws for establishing Judiciary Powers.

He has made Judges dependent on his Will alone, for the Tenure of their Offices, and the Amount and Payment of their Salaries.

He has erected a Multitude of new Offices, and sent hither Swarms of Officers to harrass our People, and eat out their Substance.

He has kept among us, in Times of Peace, Standing Armies, without the consent of our Legislatures.

He has affected to render the Military independent of and superior to the Civil Power.

He has combined with others to subject us to a Jurisdiction foreign to our Constitution, and unacknowledged by our Laws; giving his Assent to their Acts of pretended Legislation:

For quartering large Bodies of Armed Troops among us:

For protecting them, by a mock Trial, from Punishment for any Murders which they should commit on the Inhabitants of these States:

For cutting off our Trade with all Parts of the World:

For imposing Taxes on us without our Consent:

For depriving us, in many Cases, of the Benefits of Trial by Jury:

For transporting us beyond Seas to be tried for pretended Offences:

For abolishing the free System of English Laws in a neighbouring Province, establishing therein an arbitrary Government, and enlarging its Boundaries, so as to render it at once an Example and fit Instrument for introducing the same absolute Rule into these Colonies:

For taking away our Charters, abolishing our most valuable Laws, and altering fundamentally the Forms of our Governments:

For suspending our own Legislatures, and declaring themselves invested with Power to legislate for us in all Cases whatsoever.

He has abdicated Government here, by declaring us out of his Protection and waging War against us.

He has plundered our Seas, ravaged our Coasts, burnt our Towns, and destroyed the Lives of our People.

He is, at this Time, transporting large Armies of foreign Mercenaries to compleat the Works of Death, Desolation, and Tyranny, already begun with circumstances of Cruelty and Perfidy, scarcely paralleled in the most barbarous Ages, and totally unworthy the Head of a civilized Nation.

He has constrained our fellow Citizens taken Captive on the high Seas to bear Arms against their Country, to become the Executioners of their Friends and Brethren, or to fall themselves by their Hands.

He has excited domestic Insurrections amongst us, and has endeavoured to bring on the Inhabitants of our Frontiers, the merciless Indian Savages, whose known Rule of Warfare, is an undistinguished Destruction, of all Ages, Sexes and Conditions.

In every stage of these Oppressions we have Petitioned for Redress in the most humble Terms: Our repeated Petitions have been answered only by repeated Injury. A Prince, whose Character is thus marked by every act which may define a Tyrant, is unfit to be the Ruler of a free People.

Nor have we been wanting in Attentions to our British Brethren. We have warned them from Time to Time of Attempts by their Legislature to extend an unwarrantable Jurisdiction over us. We have reminded them of the Circumstances of our Emigration and Settlement here. We have appealed to their native Justice and Magnanimity, and we have conjured them by the Ties of our common Kindred to disavow these Usurpations, which, would inevitably interrupt our Connections and Correspondence. They too have been deaf to the Voice of Justice and of Consanguinity. We must, therefore, acquiesce in the Necessity, which denounces our Separation, and hold them, as we hold the rest of Mankind, Enemies in War, in Peace, Friends.

We, therefore, the Representatives of the UNITED STATES OF AMERICA, in GENERAL CONGRESS, Assembled, appealing to the Supreme Judge of the World for the Rectitude of our Intentions, do, in the Name, and by Authority of the good People of these Colonies, solemnly Publish and Declare, That these United Colonies are, and of Right ought to be, FREE AND INDEPENDENT STATES; that they are absolved from all Allegiance to the British Crown, and that all political Connection between them and the State of Great-Britain, is and ought to be totally dissolved; and that as FREE AND INDEPENDENT STATES, they have full Power to levy War, conclude Peace, contract Alliances, establish Commerce, and to do all other Acts and Things which INDEPENDENT STATES may of right do. And for the support of this Declaration, with a firm Reliance on the Protection of divine Providence, we mutually pledge to each other our Lives, our Fortunes, and our sacred Honor.

*Signed by Order and in Behalf of the Congress,*

## JOHN HANCOCK, PRESIDENT.

ATTEST.
CHARLES THOMSON, SECRETARY.

PHILADELPHIA: PRINTED BY JOHN DUNLAP.

*The American Declaration of Independence inspired portions of the United Nations' Universal Declaration of Human Rights.*

nations and their citizens have a long history of **democracy**; therefore, they think of human rights as rights that protect individual persons from actions by the state. They are concerned especially that the rights of minorities in society be protected against actions taken by the majority. **Developing nations**, however, think of human rights more in terms of **economic** and **cultural** rights. In nations that struggle with poverty, disease, and famine, people are more concerned that families, tribes, or villages have rights that enable the group to survive. In other words, developing nations emphasize the needs of groups rather than those of individuals within a larger group. Furthermore, developing nations emphasize that basic survival needs such as food, clean water, safe shelter, work, and medicines are the most important rights, while citizens of more prosperous and technologically advanced nations sometimes take such rights for granted.

## What the Universal Declaration of Human Rights Says

The General Assembly of the United Nations adopted the UDHR on December 10, 1948. The first article begins, "All human beings are born free and equal in dignity and rights. They are endowed with reason and conscience and should act towards one another in a spirit of brotherhood." Twenty-nine more articles follow. Article 2 affirms that the rights of the UDHR apply to persons of every "race, colour, sex, language, religion, political or other opinion, national or social origin, property, birth or other status." Article 3 echoes the U.S. Declaration of Independence, defending a **universal** "right to life, liberty and security of person." Article 4 states, "No one shall be held in slavery or servitude," and Article 5 says, "No one shall be subjected to torture or to cruel, inhuman or degrading treatment or punishment." The UDHR is concerned not only with physical freedom but intellectual and spiritual freedom as well. Article 18, for example, affirms, "Everyone has the right to freedom of thought, conscience and religion."

Of the thirty articles in the UDHR, twenty-two deal with individual rights and only six with economic or cultural rights. Critics say this reflects the predominantly Western viewpoint of those who composed the UDHR. At the time when they wrote it, many nations that now are independent were colonies ruled by other nations.

One of the more controversial articles in UDHR is article 21, which says, "Everyone has the right to take part in the government of his country, directly or through freely chosen representatives." This statement assumes that all nations must have a democratic form of government—one in which the people of a nation choose their own leaders. For North Americans and Europeans, this seems obvious; yet not all cultures share such confidence in democracy. Around the world, **indigenous** cultures hold traditions in which chieftains or kings assume power based on their

*The UN building in New York City*

family background, religious rituals, or other traditions. Do the framers of the UDHR have a right to declare such traditions unimportant? Critics of the West point out that democracies have begun wars, oppressed their own minorities, and taken over other nations for colonies: so what reason is there to force democracy on other nations as a superior form of government? (What do you think? This might be a good question for a discussion with your family members or with your class.)

## The International Bill of Human Rights

The UDHR is the UN's most important document regarding human rights, and it was the first international document in history that defined human rights. Therefore, it is of great political, cultural, and historical importance. However, members of the United Nations have written other documents regarding human rights. Some of these are included in the International Bill of Human Rights.

The International Bill of Human Rights is a collection of shorter documents, and all member nations of the United Nations have not yet approved it. Portions of the International Bill of Human Rights include:
- the International Covenant on Civil and Political Rights (ICCPR)
- the International Covenant on Economic, Social and Cultural Rights (ICESCR)
- the Optional Protocol to the International Covenant on Civil and Political Rights
- the Optional Protocol to the International Covenant on Civil and Political Rights aiming at the abolition of the Death Penalty.

The United Nations works to ensure justice for the people from nations around the world.

# The UN Human Rights System

Think about one of your favorite movies. It may tell a story about the fight between good and evil; in the end, criminals receive punishment for the ways they have hurt others. We like stories like that because we all want to see justice done—for ourselves and for other people.

Auschwitz was one of the most terrible of the German concentration camps.

# Crimes Against Humanity

The Nuremburg Tribunal Charter defined "crimes against humanity." These include:

- murder
- extermination
- enslavement
- deportation
- inhumane acts committed against any civilian population

In your home, your parents see to it that people treat you fairly; in your school, the teachers help keep the rules, and in your city, the courts punish wrongdoers. What if these authorities did not exist, or did not work right? Where would you go for justice?

The United Nations has organized people and committees to help the people of the world enjoy the human rights that it has promised them. The United Nations is a very complicated organization; even adults who are interested in politics have trouble figuring it all out.

## The Nuremburg Trials Lead to International Criminal Courts

For an example of international justice, the United Nations looked to the Nuremburg Trials, in which German leaders from the Second World War received judgment for their crimes against humanity. You might have seen movies or heard people talk about the Holocaust, which happened during World War II. The Holocaust was one of the worst things that ever happened in the world; German soldiers, under the direction of Adolf Hitler, killed millions of people held in prison camps. These women, children, and men had done nothing wrong to the government or other people. The German government killed them because of their race, their religion, their sexual orientation, or physical or mental disabilities.

Eventually, the United States, Britain, and other nations defeated the German army and freed the prisoners who were still alive in these camps. Some of the top German leaders, including Hitler, had killed themselves or died in the war, but many other Nazi officials were captured. The Allies had to decide how to deal with the Nazi murderers. They formed a court of law made up of people from several different nations to pass judgment and punish the Nazi criminals.

The court followed procedures modeled after U.S. and British courts, and a panel of judges from the United States, Britain, and the Soviet Union tried the ***defendants***. The Nuremberg cases were the first time leaders of a nation faced justice from the international community for their wartime actions. The defendants faced accusations of waging a war of aggression, war crimes, and crimes against humanity. Accusations like these have since become common in international law.

Most of the Nazi leaders claimed they did not know about the ***pogrom*** of mass murders of people considered "undesirable," or they said they were innocent because they followed orders from higher authorities. Their testimonies provided the world with horrid details of the Holocaust and other terrible things done by the Nazis. Twelve defendants received the death sentence, seven received long prison terms, and three were acquitted (declared not guilty). The Nuremberg Trials prepared the way for later international war crimes prosecutions and the International Criminal Court (ICC).

After the end of the Cold War (the rivalry between the United States and Soviet Union that lasted from the 1950s through the 1970s), the United Nations created courts to deal with crimes against humanity. The UN Security Council established the International Criminal Tribunal for the Former Yugoslavia in 1993, with headquarters in The Hague. They also formed the International Criminal Tribunal for Rwanda in 1994, based in Arusha, Tanzania. These courts expressed the horror of the world at the genocide (the deliberate slaughter of entire large groups of people) that took place during crises in these countries.

In addition to the courts noted above, as of 2005, the United Nations has established several other international courts. One is the Special Court for Sierra Leone (SCSL): during Sierra Leone's brutal civil war, rebels terrorized civilians with amputation (cutting off body parts) and rape; the

## Human Rights Commissioners of Note

The first person to hold the post of UN High Commissioner of Human Rights was José Ayala Lasso, a former foreign minister from Ecuador; Mary Robinson, the former president of Ireland, followed him. Vieira de Mello assumed the job on September 12, 2002, before the United Nations asked him to serve as its envoy to Iraq: there, terrorist bombers killed him along with twenty-one other victims. In 2004, the General Assembly approved the appointment of Justice Louise Arbour of Canada as UN High Commissioner for Human Rights. She formerly served as Canadian Supreme Court Justice and prosecutor of UN war crimes tribunals for the former Yugoslavia and Rwanda.

*The Hague's Peace Palace houses the principal judicial body of the United Nations, the International Court of Justice.*

SCSL is an international court working to bring the people who committed these crimes to justice. Another is the Special Tribunal for Cambodia: during the 1970s, the Khmer Rouge (Cambodian ***communist*** fighters) killed more than 1 million people; thirty years later, the United Nations and the Cambodian government agreed to form an international court to try those responsible for these deaths. Yet another international criminal court is the Ad-Hoc Court for Timor-Leste: during Timor's struggle for independence, pro-Indonesia ***militias*** backed by the Indonesian government murdered approximately 1,300 to 2,000 Timorese and caused 300,000 to become refugees. The Ad-Hoc Court for Timor-Leste hoped to provide justice for victims' families, but trials could not go forward because the Indonesian government does not recognize the court and refuses to hand over accused persons.

In 1998, a conference of one hundred nations established the ICC, which came into official existence on July 1, 2002. The ICC is a permanent court, unlike the temporary courts established by the United Nations to judge cases related to specific situations and nations. The ICC is not part of the United Nations, yet it prosecutes cases of serious crimes that concern the international community. Because it claims authority in matters of international law and functions apart from the United Nations, the ICC is a new direction in international law concerning human rights.

# UNICEF and Other Human Rights Efforts: Protecting Individuals

## The Human Rights Committee

You should not confuse the Human Rights Committee (HRC) with the UN Commission on Human Rights, created in 1946 to draft the UDHR. The United Nations established the HRC in 1976. The committee meets three times each year in either New York or Geneva to look at reports on human rights in nations that have signed the International Covenant on Civil and Political Rights. The International Covenant is an agreement formed in 1966, which makes up part of the International Bill of Human Rights. As of 2005, 149 member states have signed that they agree with the International Covenant. It details freedoms of speech, press, worship, ***assembly***, security of person and property, political participation, ***due process***, and protection against unreasonable government action. The HRC receives national reports on the status of rights listed in the covenant. Its members discuss these reports with national representatives and make confidential recommendations to the national governments.

*The tribal people of Africa are especially vulnerable to human rights violations.*

## High Commissioner for Human Rights

In June 1993, representatives of 171 UN member states agreed on the Vienna Declaration, a common plan for strengthening human rights around the world. This was the result of an important two-week-long world conference. Seven thousand participants took part in the conference, including teachers, politicians, and representatives of more than eight hundred NGOs. Participants talked about how various forms of human rights—political, economic, social, and cultural—relate to each other. They agreed the entire world community has an obligation to help poorer nations develop economically. The Vienna Declaration also emphasized the rights of vulnerable groups, especially women and indigenous peoples (for example, American Indians in the United States or Zulu tribal people in South Africa). At the conference, UN secretary-general at the time, Boutros Boutros-Ghali, congratulated members for creating "a new vision for global action for human rights into the next century."

One part of the Vienna Declaration was the creation of the position of UN High Commissioner for Human Rights (UNHCHR). The UNHCHR stands up for human rights and coordinates UN programs, offices, and agencies dealing with human rights. The UN Centre for Human Rights is one of the most important offices under the UNHCHR. The Centre is located in Geneva, Switzerland, and provides suggestions and information for all the other programs, offices, and agencies under the UNHCHR.

In December of 2005, Human Rights Commissioner Louise Arbour expressed concern over claims that the U.S. government had secret jails in other countries. She said governments must reveal if they are holding prisoners in secret jails. Arbour said she wanted to inspect any such centers. She wondered if the U.S. government, in its efforts to fight against terrorists, was following the rules the UN member states had agreed on to eliminate torture in the world. John Bolton, the U.S. envoy to the United Nations, said her comments were "inappropriate," but Arbour said she had to protect and defend human rights, and she would continue to do that: "I'm the United Nations High Commissioner for Human Rights. This is what I do."

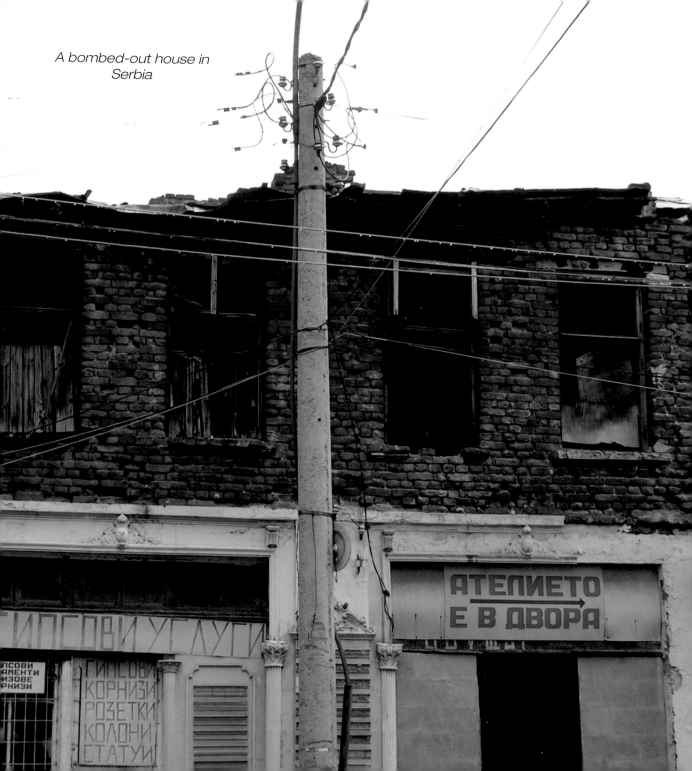
A bombed-out house in Serbia

# 5

# Human Rights and International Law

W hen she was twelve years old, Edima spent her days with her mother, poking through ruined buildings looking for scraps of food so they would not starve. Occasionally, shots would ring out, and they would hide from Serbian soldiers who were trying to kill them. Other times, grenades or cannon shells exploded near them.

*Portrait of Hugo Grotius*

## A Man Whose Ideas Were Centuries Ahead of His Time

Dutchman Hugo Grotius (1583-1645) created the idea of international law. In 1625, Grotius published *De jure belli ac pacis* (*Concerning the law of war and peace*), the first serious attempt to write laws for use between nations. Grotius was both a lawyer and a theologian (a scholar who studies God) and lived at a time when Europeans killed each other because of their differing religious beliefs. Grotius believed that faith in God should lead nations to work together, rather than kill each other. At the time of his death, Grotius was bitter because people had not listened to his ideas; Europeans were still fighting religious wars. Grotius' dying words were, "I have spent my life laboriously doing nothing." However, after his death, politicians and students from many nations became interested in Grotius' ideas. His book was a seed that grew into the many international laws that exist today.

This was a daily routine in Sarajevo, the capital of Bosnia, in 1993—and yet shooting or bombing children and women is against the rules of international law, the rules agreed to by most nations of the world.

## History and Philosophy of International Law

Throughout human history, there have been formal statements between tribes, kingdoms, and nations that list the behaviors on which the nations can all agree. As travel and communication improved, growing discussions between nations led to what some lawyers and politicians regarded as "international law." Usually, international law dealt with **embassies**, **ambassadors**, and other matters directly involving relations between nations.

Since the time when the United Nations was established, people from the various nations have held differing opinions about what international law is and how nations should follow it. According to one view, all nations should obey international law just as individuals should obey the laws of their own nations. However, some thinkers, including former U.S. secretary of state Henry Kissinger, have argued there really is no such thing as international law because laws are meaningless if no one makes sure that nations are following them. People who hold this perspective argue that all nations create rules that work for their own needs so no one can create fair international laws. Some Chinese scholars say international laws actually work for wealthy Western

*Different cultures have different values, so it is difficult to create rules that apply to everyone.*

nations at the expense of poorer less developed nations. Feminists (people concerned for women's rights) argue that international law codes work for men at the expense of women throughout the nations. Philosophers have recently challenged the possibility of a moral system that works for all people; they argue that people in different cultures are too different to allow a "one size fits all" set of rules.

Despite all those problems, most nations today recognize that international laws are important. In many cases, it is impossible to enforce international laws, but when they are enforced, it is often by means of economic sanctions (in which nations refuse to do business with other nations), which usually harm most those who can least afford it. The growing importance of international law in recent years is in part due to the actions of the United Nations.

## The International Law Commission (ILC)

The Charter of the United Nations directs the General Assembly to "initiate studies and make recommendations" in order to promote the growth of international law. To fulfill this, the General

*International laws that protect the rights of men do not always offer women the same protection.*

*Eleanor Roosevelt led the UN Commission on Human Rights when it wrote the Universal Declaration of Human Rights.*

Assembly in 1947 voted to create the International Law Commission (ILC). The ILC first met June 17, 1948. Its task is to promote the principles of the UN Charter through means of expanding international law.

The ILC began with only fifteen members and has since expanded to thirty-four members. Each member must be an expert in the field of international law. Members serve for five-year terms, and no two may come from the same nation. By 2001, the ILC had completed documents on nineteen topics and was working on five more. In 1992, the ILC began working on a suggestion for the establishment of the ICC; that suggestion led to the 1998 Rome conference and subsequent formation of the ICC.

## UN Influence on Human Rights in International Law

In 1946, the Economic and Social Council of the United Nations (ECOSOC) established the UN Commission on Human Rights. American first lady Eleanor Roosevelt led this group as it wrote the UDHR. It was a truly multicultural project: Peng-chung Chang from China was an Asian who followed the beliefs taught by Confucius (a Chinese philosopher who lived five centuries before the Christian era of history); Charles Malik was a Middle Eastern Arab; Hernan Santa Cruz from Chile helped the committee understand how Latin Americans thought about human rights issues; and René Cassin, a French Jew, contributed insights from the Jewish people in Europe, who had just come through the Holocaust. Because they came from different countries, cultures, and religions, the members of the commission were better able to write a document that expressed the views of all peoples of the world.

A house in Gambia

# The United Nations in Action

When Lamin Sise was a boy, his country, Gambia, was a colony belonging to the United Kingdom (Britain). British governors made Gambian laws and told teachers what they must teach in Gambia's schools. When the British queen visited Gambia, Lamin and other children waved British flags as she rode down the streets. Lamin remembers the day when people from the United Nations came to his village, telling the people they could decide for themselves what kind of government they wanted to have. Not long after that, Lamin and other Gambians had a flag and government of their own: Gambia had achieved independence.

## UNICEF's Work in Gambia

UNICEF has worked diligently to improve life in Gambia. It has developed programs in HIV/AIDS education, arranged and early marriages, teenage pregnancy, and violence against women and girls. UNICEF has worked with civil organizations to increase enrollment and retention of girls in school. The Baby-Friendly Community Initiative promotes breastfeeding of infants until the age of six months.

## In Action for Independence: Namibia and Timor-Leste

Human rights include the right to independence, to live freely under a government chosen by its people. According to *The United Nations 50th Anniversary Book*, "The UN doesn't decide what form of government a country should have. It helps make sure that the people are free to decide for themselves. One of the goals of the UN is to help colonies become independent nations." In 1946, when the UN was founded, more than half the people of the world lacked this right; they lived in colonies. During the past sixty years, the United Nations has helped fifty-three countries gain independence from colonialism. Historians say that during this time more countries achieved independence without having to go to war than ever before.

Today, some 1.5 million people live in sixteen "non-self-governing territories." The largest of these is Western Sahara, an area approximately the size of Colorado. The smallest is Pitcairn Island, with a population of forty-six people in an area just over a square mile. These non-self-governing territories are places that do not live under their own government; rather, the UN Trusteeship Council oversees all these areas.

Since 1966, the African nation of Namibia had been under the care of the United Nations, although the country of South Africa occupied it. While Namibia was under UN care, the United Nations took legal actions to protect Namibia's interests and cooperated with Namibia's liberation movement, the South West Africa People's Organization (SWAPO). Finally, UN efforts achieved

*"The most important meaning of this Nobel award is the solemn recognition that the welfare of today's children is inseparably linked with the peace of tomorrow's world."*
—Henry R. Labouisse, executive director of UNICEF (1965–1979), in his acceptance of the Nobel Peace Prize in 1965 on behalf of UNICEF.

## UNICEF in Namibia

UNICEF joined with the Emergency Management Unit and World Food Programme to perform a vulnerability assessment of the Namibian people, especially its children and women. It has also worked with the Ministry of Health and Social Services and the Catholic Health Services to undertake emergency nutrition support targeting severely malnourished young children in the worst-affected areas.

an agreement regarding Namibia's independence. The United Nations oversaw free elections and withdrawal of South African forces from Namibia, and on March 21, 1990, Namibia began its new life as an independent nation.

The most recent nation to gain independence is Timor-Leste; this new nation is also an outstanding example of UN success. Timor-Leste was a Portuguese colony from 1509 until 1974,

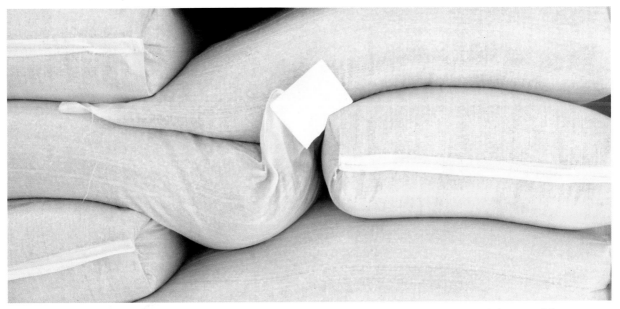

*Sacks of grain wait to be distributed to famine-stricken regions of the world.*

## UNICEF in Timor-Leste

UNICEF continues to have a presence in Timor-Leste. The organization runs a vaccination campaign, repairs water systems, provides medical aid and supplies, enhances nutrition, and works to improve the educational system.

when Portugal granted the nation independence. However, the following year Indonesia invaded Timor-Leste and declared it the twenty-seventh Indonesian province; they did not consult the Timor-Leste people about their wishes. For the next two decades, Timor-Leste patriots fought a *guerrilla war* with the Indonesian army. During that conflict, the Indonesia army and their supporters killed more than 100,000 Timor-Leste people; many of these deaths occurred because

*Many blacks in South Africa live in communities where the houses are made of tin, while whites often have more money.*

## UNICEF in El Salvador

UNICEF's work in El Salvador focuses on the national and the local levels. Programs at the national level include those that promote children's rights legislation.

On the local level, UNICEF is working for programs that will provide safety for children at the more immediate level. The goal of these programs is to reduce the causes that can make children vulnerable and lead to a violation of their rights. Under the program Child-Friendly Municipalities, UNICEF is working with local officials and organizations to increase awareness about children's rights.

UNICEF is also involved in a pilot program to reduce violence in schools, a serious problem in El Salvador. Students learn conflict management and other ways to solve problems.

Indonesian forces destroyed homes, hospitals, farms, and transportation. In 1999, the United Nations helped the Timor-Leste people vote to become an independent nation, but the Indonesian army and its supporters took revenge before leaving Timor-Leste: they killed thousands of Timor-Leste civilians or forced them to become refugees; and they destroyed cities, power plants, bridges, and government buildings. In 2002, UN forces came into the country to protect the Timor-Leste people, and Timor-Leste finally became free. As of 2005, a small UN force remains in Timor-Leste to protect and help rebuild the country.

## Action for Equal Rights: South Africa

The Republic of South Africa formed in 1910; it consisted of British settlers, Dutch settlers called Afrikaners, and native Africans who were the majority of the nation's people. White South Africans imposed a strict system of *segregation* on the black majority. Called apartheid ("apartness" in Dutch), this policy restricted blacks in terms of interracial marriage, work, education, housing, travel, voting, and access to medical care.

There were many ways that the system of apartheid caused pain and suffering for black people in South Africa. For example, children in black South African schools often had no books or school supplies, while white schoolchildren enjoyed plenty of educational supplies. Some black people died because their segregated communities did not have good hospitals, ambulances, or doctors. Black South Africans tried to organize themselves and protest this unfair situation, but

# UNICEF and Other Human Rights Efforts: Protecting Individuals

## UNICEF in South Africa

In South Africa, UNICEF's priorities center on education and health care. South Africa has an extremely high HIV/AIDS rate. UNICEF is working to educate the citizens of South Africa about HIV/AIDS prevention.

UNICEF is also working to provide training in and care of persons living with HIV/AIDS. It also works on behalf of children who are orphaned or otherwise affected by the disease, helping them receive their rights.

Education in general is a major recipient of UNICEF assistance. UNICEF is developing programs to provide educational opportunities to all, and to help student retention.

government officers fought against them and many were jailed. One of the best known of the protesters is Nelson Mandela, who was jailed for life in 1964 for the crime of sabotage; he was released in 1990 and was later elected president of South Africa.

The United Nations protested apartheid from the time the world body began. In 1960, the Sharpesville Massacre brought apartheid to even greater world attention when a group of white South African police officers opened fire on a group of unarmed black protesters, killing seventy protesters and wounding more than a hundred. In 1977, the United Nations banned South Africa

## UNICEF in Bosnia

UNICEF's efforts in Bosnia center on health care and education. Through programs sponsored by UNICEF, doctors and nurses have been trained on the benefits of breast-feeding. UNICEF has helped medical facilities obtain needed vaccines for such diseases as tuberculosis, diphtheria, and hepatitis B. The Mine Risk Education program, sponsored by UNICEF, has increased awareness of land mines. As a result, the number of deaths and injuries due to them has been reduced significantly.

Education has also benefited by UNICEF's work. In a coordinated effort with other organizations, UNICEF is helping to train teachers in better, more modern methods of teaching. UNICEF has also persuaded the government to become more active in the education of Roma and other minority group children.

*Houses in Bosnia still bear the scars of war.*

from all General Assembly activities, and the UN Security Council voted for an ***arms embargo*** against South Africa. In the following years, more embargos cut off supplies of foreign investments, cultural exchanges, international sports participation, and trade. This hurt the country considerably at a time when South Africa was spending a quarter of its national budget to support apartheid. In the early 1990s, Simon Brand, chairman of the South African Development bank, noted, "Apartheid is a monkey on the back of the economy. It is suffocating us."

Finally, pressures put on South Africa by the United Nations combined with the freedom movement of black South Africans to achieve the end of apartheid. The South African government agreed in 1993 to allow black South Africans equal rights and an equal voice in their country's future, and South Africa held its first multiracial national elections the following year.

## Decade-Late Regrets

In July of 2004, UN Secretary-General Kofi Annan spoke to the Commission on Human Rights gathered at the Assembly Hall of the Palais des Nations in Geneva, Switzerland, at a special meeting to observe the International Day of Reflection on the 1994 genocide in Rwanda. He said:

We must never forget our collective failure to protect at least eight hundred thousand defenseless men, women and children who perished in Rwanda ten years ago. Such crimes cannot be reversed. Such failures cannot be repaired. The dead cannot be brought back to life. So what can we do? First, we must all acknowledge our responsibility for not having done more to prevent or stop the genocide. Neither the United Nations Secretariat, nor the Security Council, nor Member States in general, nor the international media, paid enough attention to the gathering signs of disaster. Still less did we take timely action. When we recall such events and ask "why did no one intervene?" we should address the question not only to the United Nations, or even to its Member States. No one can claim ignorance. All who were playing any part in world affairs at that time should ask, "what more could I have done? How would I react next time—and what am I doing now to make it less likely there will be a next time?"

## Attempts to Defend Human Rights: El Salvador, Bosnia, and Rwanda

While the end of apartheid in South African and independence of Timor-Leste illustrate the UN's ability to achieve positive results in the world, the late twentieth century also provided examples of its inability to defend people against death and torture. In 1993, the United Nations released a report disapproving of the way the Salvadoran military government tortured and killed its civilians. El Salvador reacted to the report by releasing military officers accused of human rights abuses—hardly the response the United Nations had hoped for!

As far as critics were concerned, the United Nations was doing too little too late. For more than two decades prior to the report, there had been a widespread pattern of human rights abuses in El Salvador. By 1990, fighting and rights abuses had claimed more than 75,000 Salvadoran lives. According to the Web site of the Farabundo Marti National Liberation (FMNL), the group that opposed the Salvadoran government in the civil war and is now the leading political party in the country:

Agreement was reached in July 1990 that the United Nations monitor rights violations after a ceasefire. UN-sponsored negotiations continued, and on January 16, 1992, a peace accord was signed between the government and guerilla groups. A ceasefire went into effect on February 1. Under the agreement, the Salvadorian army was to be sharply reduced, the guerilla forces were to be absorbed into Salvadorian society, a new national police was to be created, and *land reform* measures enacted. In 1992, reconstruction began, under which the guerillas returned to civilian life in return for economic, social, and political reforms.

*The peaceful landscape in Rwanda does not reveal the violence and injustice that took place here.*

# UNICEF and Other Human Rights Efforts: Protecting Individuals

In the end, the United Nations did help end the horrors of civil war and human rights abuses in El Salvador, but critics accused the organization of being ***passive*** for a long time while those abuses went on. Some politicians and thinkers believe the United Nations is overly reluctant to interfere in nations' affairs when people within a nation are suffering. The situation in Bosnia provided another example of a "too little, too late" response to a dire human rights tragedy.

In the Republic of Bosnia-Herzegovina, fighting between three ethnic groups, the Serbs, Croats, and Muslims, resulted in genocide committed by the Serbs against the Muslims. Bosnia is one of several small countries that emerged from the breakup of Yugoslavia, a country composed of ethnic and religious groups that had been historical enemies. In the late 1980s, the Serbian leader Slobodan Milosevic used nationalism and religious hatred to gain power by inflaming tensions between Serbs and Muslims in the independent province of Kosovo. In 1991, Slovenia and Croatia declared their independence from Yugoslavia, resulting in civil war. Milosevic's forces

## UNICEF in Rwanda

UNICEF's priorities in Rwanda include:

1. reduce morbidity and mortality of children under age five and reduce maternal mortality by 25 percent,
2. make primary education available to all children, and
3. protect all children, with an emphasis on those with special needs, from exploitation and abuse.

Programs such as those designed to reduce the transmission of HIV/AIDS from mother to child and a malaria control program have reduced morbidity and mortality. Health-care programs in nutrition and hygiene have also aided in improved health of children and adults. The water and sanitation component supports water quality management, hygiene, sanitation and community environmental care through schools and policy development.

Teacher-training, curriculum development, and elimination of exploitative labor projects are three ways UNICEF has helped improve the educational system, especially for girls.

UNICEF continues to serve as an advocate for those who need special protection. These include imprisoned youth, orphans, and children with special physical or psychological needs.

*A skull gives witness to Rwanda's genocide.*

## UNICEF in Darfur

UNICEF is working with other agencies to provide humanitarian aid to those in need. These organizations are working to improve water and environmental sanitation; health care and nutrition, including vaccination and health-care worker training programs; education, including the construction of more than 1,500 temporary classrooms; and child protection, including reporting rape and gender-based violence and serving as an advocate for children.

invaded Croatia to "protect" the Serbian minority. During that invasion, the Serbs began the first mass executions of the conflict, killing hundreds of Croats and burying them in mass graves. Then, in 1992, the United States and Europe recognized the independence of Bosnia; Milosevic responded to Bosnia's declaration of independence by attacking Sarajevo, its capital city. In Sarajevo, Serb snipers shot down helpless civilians in the streets, eventually killing more than 3,500 children. As the Serb army moved into Bosnia, they engaged in *ethnic cleansing*, including mass shootings, *forced repopulation* of entire towns, confinement in makeshift concentration camps, and using rape as a weapon against women and girls.

Eventually, the United Nations did get involved, but they did little to change the ghastly situation. The United Nations imposed economic sanctions on Serbia and *deployed* its troops to help distribute food and medicine to dispossessed Muslims, but the United Nations did not allow its troops to fight against the Serbs; they remained neutral throughout 1993 at a time when Serbs in Bosnia committed genocide against Muslims. Bosnian Serbs even attacked the UN peacekeepers; they took UN peacekeepers as hostages and turned them into human shields, chaining them to military targets. UN peacekeepers stood by helplessly as Serbs slaughtered nearly 8,000 men and boys, the worst mass murder in Europe since World War II. Furthermore, the Serbs continued to engage in mass rapes of Muslim women.

Finally, in 1995, the United States, under the leadership of President Bill Clinton, led a full-scale military campaign of NATO (North Atlantic Treaty Organization) troops, effectively ending the mass slaughter by the Serbs. By the time NATO intervened, Serbs had murdered over 200,000 Bosnian Muslim civilians and 2 million had become refugees. It was, according to U.S. assistant secretary of state Richard Holbrooke, "The greatest failure of the West since the 1930s." Alas, it was not the only failure by the United Nations to prevent human rights abuses in the 1990s; Rwanda provided another grim lesson in UN ineffectiveness.

*Children wait in line in Darfur.*

*The Earth is a fragile home to millions of human beings—and wars and violence
threaten its peace.*

Two ethnic groups—the Hutus and the Tutsis—populate Rwanda. During the years when Rwanda was a Belgian colony, the Belgians encouraged divisions between the two groups. Beginning in 1990, the Rwandan Patriotic Front (RPF) fought to overthrow the Hutu-led Rwandan government, and in 1993, 2,500 UN troops moved into Rwanda to enforce peace between the warring parties. In January 1994, General Romeo Dallaire, commander of the peacekeepers, warned the United Nations that Hutus were preparing to massacre Tutsis. On April 7, Hutu militiamen began slaughtering Tutsis; they also tortured and killed ten Belgian UN peacekeepers in the hope of persuading Belgium to remove its troops. Two weeks later, the UN Security Council voted to withdraw all but a small number of troops, exactly as the Hutu militia hoped they would. The Tutsi RPF fought to take back the country, eventually succeeding, but not before the Hutus killed 800,000 Tutsis. In April of 2000, the UN Security Council accepted responsibility for failing to prevent the 1994 genocide in Rwanda. Council members admitted their governments had lacked the political will to stop the massacres.

## The UN and Human Rights in the Twenty-First Century

At the end of 2005, a dire situation existed in the Darfur region of western Sudan, Africa. This conflict began in 2003, when two rebel groups attacked the Sudanese government. In response to the rebels, militia forces called Janjaweed committed gross violations of human rights against defenseless civilians of the same ethnic groups as the rebels. As of December 2005, observers estimated that the Janjaweed had killed more than 50,000 people and driven one million from their homes.

Once again, critics were frustrated that the United Nations had not taken an effective response to these grave violations of human rights. A December 8, 2005, article in the *Sudan Tribune* lamented:

Unless a strengthened peacekeeping force is put in place in war-torn Darfur, Sudan, thousands more Sudanese may perish over the coming months . . . security has deteriorated to such an alarming degree that aid agencies are finding it ever more difficult to provide assistance. We may soon face disastrous consequences. . . . The international community must urgently do all it can to help stabilize the security situation before all humanitarian assistance becomes untenable. Specifically, a larger and more robust peace-monitoring or peacekeeping presence in Darfur—whether under African Union or United Nations auspices—is absolutely essential.

Although the United Nations has often failed to protect human rights, it continues its fight to improve the lives of people around the globe.

Peter Takirambudde, executive director of Human Rights Watch Africa Division, was critical of the limited UN response to the situation, claiming the Security Council's response fell far short of that needed to end the atrocities in Darfur. Takirambudde said, "The Security Council will be judged harshly by history. . . . The resolution on Darfur is a pitiful response to ongoing murder, rape and ethnic cleansing."

## Uncertain Future

For more than a decade, the United Nations has proven ineffective in preventing catastrophic abuses of human rights; therefore, an increasing number of politicians, especially in the United States, are questioning whether the organization can fulfill its purposes in coming years. However, over the longer course of its history, the United Nations has done important work in creating rules governing international human rights, and in a number of cases, it has managed to improve people's lives.

# Time Line

| | |
|---|---|
| 1215 | Magna Carta is signed. |
| 1625 | Hugo Grotius publishes *De jure belli ac pacis*. |
| 1815 | Congress of Vienna is held. |
| 1907 | The Hague Convention is held. |
| 1919 | League of Nations is formed. |
| 1938 | The Holocaust begins. |
| 1941 | Inter-Allied Declaration is drafted in London. |
| 1943 | U.S. secretary of state Cordell Hull proposes Charter for the United Nations. |
| 1945 | Nuremburg trials of Nazi war criminals are held. |
| October 24, 1945 | The UN Charter is approved. |
| 1946 | UN Commission on Human Rights is formed. |
| 1947 | International Law Commission is formed. |
| 1948 | Universal Declaration of Human Rights is adopted. |
| 1959 | Declaration of the Rights of the Child is adopted. |
| 1966 | International Covenant on Civil and Political Rights is adopted. |
| 1977 | South Africa is banned from General Assembly. |
| 1990 | Namibia achieves independence. |

| | |
|---|---|
| 1992 | El Salvador peace accord ends mass killings. |
| 1993 | Apartheid ends in South Africa. |
| 1993 | Vienna Declaration on Human Rights is adopted. |
| 1993 | Genocide occurs in Bosnia. |
| 1993 | International Criminal Tribunal for the Former Yugoslavia is established. |
| 1994 | Genocide occurs in Rwanda. |
| 1994 | José Ayala Lasso becomes the first UN High Commissioner for Human Rights. |
| 1998 | International Criminal Court forms. |
| 2002 | Timor-Leste is granted independence. |
| 2004 | Commemoration of Rwanda genocide is held. |
| 2005 | Mass killings take place in Sudan. |
| 2006 | The United Nations continues to work to protect human rights around the world. |

# Glossary

*Allied:* Referring to the forces that joined together to fight Germany and its allies in World War I and against the Axis powers in World War II.

*ambassadors:* Diplomatic officials of the highest rank sent by one country to serve as its long-term representatives in another country or to an international organization.

*arms embargo:* Government restrictions on the trade of firearms.

*assembly:* The coming together of people for a common purpose.

*colonies:* Countries or areas that are ruled by another country.

*communist:* A supporter of communism, the political system in which all property and wealth is owned in a classless society by all members of a community.

*cultural:* Relating to a particular culture or civilization.

*defendants:* People required to answer criminal or civil charges in a court.

*democracy:* A system of government elected freely and equally by its people.

*deployed:* Positioned troops, weapons, and other resources to prepare for conflict.

*developing nations:* Nations where the average income is much lower than in industrial nations, where the economy relies on a few export crops, and where farming is conducted by primitive methods.

*discrimination:* Unfair treatment of one person or group, usually because of prejudice about race, ethnic group, age group, religion, or gender.

*due process:* The entitlement of a citizen to proper legal procedures.

*economic:* Relating to the production and consumption of goods and services of a community regarded as a whole.

**embassies:** Residences and workplaces of ambassadors, the representatives of other countries.

**ethnic cleansing:** The violent elimination or removal from an area of people attacked because of their ethnic backgrounds, by means of genocide or forced expulsion.

**famine:** A severe shortage of food resulting in widespread hunger.

**forced repopulation:** The forced removal of a group of people from an area so another group can move in.

**groundwater:** Water beneath the surface of the earth that supplies wells and springs.

**guerrilla war:** Irregular warfare conducted by independent units by means of harassment and sabotage.

**humanitarian:** Concerned about the well-being of other people.

**indigenous:** Native to an area.

**internally displaced:** Forced to leave homes or residences, in particular as a result of or in order to avoid the effects of armed conflict, situations of generalized violence, violations of human rights, or natural or human-made disasters, without crossing an internationally recognized national border.

**isolationism:** A government policy based on the belief that national interests are best served by avoiding economic and political alliances with other countries.

**land reform:** Measures designed to bring about a more equal distribution of agricultural land.

**latrines:** Communal toilets, usually on a military base.

**militias:** Citizens organized for military service.

**multicultural:** Relating to the cultures of different countries, ethnic groups, or religions.

**passive:** Tending not to participate actively and usually letting others make decisions.

**pogrom:** A government-sanctioned planned campaign of persecution or extermination directed against an ethnic group, especially against the Jewish people in Nazi Germany and in tsarist Russia.

**polio:** Poliomyelitis; a severe infectious disease that inflames the brain stem and spinal cord, sometimes leading to paralysis and muscular wasting.

**Security Council:** The permanent committee of the United Nations that oversees its worldwide peacekeeping missions.

**segregation:** The practice of keeping ethnic, racial, religious, or gender groups separate.

**standard of living:** The level of material comfort enjoyed by a person, group, or society.

**tuberculosis (TB):** An infectious disease that causes small rounded swellings to form on mucous membranes and affects the lungs.

**universal:** Relating to the whole world or everyone in the world.

# Further Reading

Brenner, Barbara. *The United Nations 50th Anniversary Book.* New York: Simon & Schuster, 1995.

Fasulo, Linda. *An Insider's Guide to the UN.* New Haven, Conn.: Yale University Press, 2004.

Jacobs, William Jay. *Search for Peace: The Story of the United Nations.* New York: Charles Scribner's Sons, 1994.

Starke, Linda, ed. *The Worldwatch Institute State of the World 2005: Redefining Global Security.* New York: W.W. Norton, 2005.

Woog, Adam. *The United Nations.* San Diego, Calif.: Lucent, 1994.

# For More Information

Bosnia Genocide: United Human Rights Council
www.unitedhumanrights.org/Genocide/bosnia_genocide.htm

Charter of the United Nations: Office of the High Commissioner of Human Rights Charter of the United Nations
www.unhchr.ch/html/menu3/b/ch-cont.htm

Children's Rights: Global Education
www.globaleducation.edna.edu.au/globaled/go/cache/offonce/pid/26

CIA: The World Factbook: Timor-Leste
www.cia.gov/cia/publications/factbook/geos/tt.html

Declaration of the Rights of the Child: Office of the High Commissioner of Human Rights Charter of the United Nations
www.unhchr.ch/html/menu3/b/25.htm

El Salvador: World Country Guide
www.travel-guide.com/data/slv/slv580.asp

United Nations Treaty Collection: untreaty.org
untreaty.un.org/english/guide.asp

Universal Declaration of Human Rights: UN.org
www.un.org/Overview/rights.html

Publisher's note:
The Web sites listed on this page were active at the time of publication. The publisher is not responsible for Web sites that have changed their addresses or discontinued operation since the date of publication. The publisher will review and update the Web-site list upon each reprint.

# Reports and Projects

**Written Reports**

Write a report about human rights for a group of people (for example, women, children, migrants).

Research news sites on the Internet and report on what the United Nations is doing this week.

Write to offices of the United Nations regarding a current issue; tell how you feel about it and ask what the United Nations is doing about that issue.

Write a suggestion on how to make the United Nations work better.

**Oral Reports/Drama/Media/Debate**

Imagine you are a citizen of Timor-Leste, Rwanda, Sudan, or another nation, and tell how the United Nations does (or does not) influence your life.

Form teams and debate the topic: "The UN does (or does not) work well to protect human rights."

Do a multimedia presentation (PowerPoint, collage, or CD/DVD with accompanying oral report) about a human rights problem today (for example, torture, poverty, slavery). Include information on how your classmates can be involved in helping to improve the situation.

Work in a group. Pretend you each represent a different continent. Together, come up with a plan to improve human rights in the twenty-first century.

Form a panel with students representing various nations. Each national representative should explain what he or she thinks is the most important human rights issue today and why.

# Bibliography

BBC News. http://www.bbc.co.uk/home/d

Moore, John Allphin, Jr., and Jerry Pubantz. *Encyclopedia of the United Nations.* New York: Facts on File, 2002.

Office of the UN High Commissioner of Human Rights. http://www.ohchr.org/english.
UN.org. Welcome to the UN.http://www.un.org.

United Human Rights Council. http://www.unitedhumanrights.org.

United Nations Treaty Collection. Treaty Reference Guide. http://untreaty.un.org/english/guide.asp, 2005.

# Index

# Picture Credits

# Biographies

Author

Roger Smith is a writer who previously spent a decade teaching junior high school in a multiethnic setting. He has traveled to the Middle East and Central America and has participated in organizations committed to world peace and human rights issues.

Series Consultant

Bruce Russett is Dean Acheson Professor of Political Science at Yale University and editor of the *Journal of Conflict Resolution*. He has taught or researched at Columbia, Harvard, M.I.T., Michigan, and North Carolina in the United States, and educational institutions in Belgium, Britain, Israel, Japan, and the Netherlands. He has been president of the International Studies Association and the Peace Science Society, holds an honorary doctorate from Uppsala University in Sweden. He was principal adviser to the U.S. Catholic Bishops for their pastoral letter on nuclear deterrence in 1985, and co-directed the staff for the 1995 Ford Foundation Report, *The United Nations in Its Second Half Century*. He has served as editor of the *Journal of Conflict Resolution* since 1973. The twenty-five books he has published include *The Once and Future Security Council* (1997), *Triangulating Peace: Democracy, Interdependence, and International Organizations* (2001), *World Politics: The Menu for Choice* (8th edition 2006), and *Purpose and Policy in the Global Community* (2006).